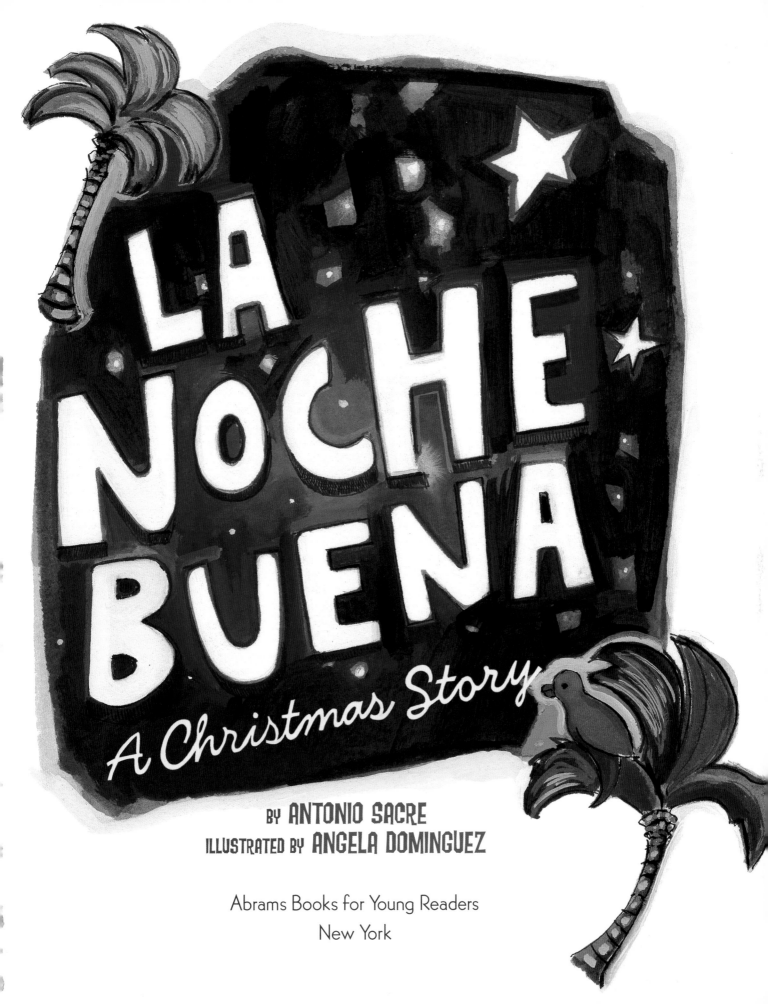

LA NOCHE BUENA

A Christmas Story

BY ANTONIO SACRE
ILLUSTRATED BY ANGELA DOMINGUEZ

Abrams Books for Young Readers
New York

WHEN I ARRIVE AT MY *ABUELA* MIMI'S HOUSE, IT IS HOT.
Too hot for making snowmen, too hot for ice-skating. Too hot for
evergreens. My *abuela*, my grandmother, lives in a neighborhood called
Little Havana, in Miami, Florida. Palm trees sway overhead. How will Santa
land his sleigh in this heat? As much as I love my Cuban grandmother, and as
many times as she tells me I'm her favorite *nieta*, granddaughter, I'd rather
be up north for Christmas, with my mother, my other grandmother, all my
up-north cousins, and snow, lots and lots of snow!

It's my dad's turn to have me, and he wants
me to see how the Cuban side of my family
celebrates the holidays. He says *La Noche Buena*,
Christmas Eve, is the best night of the year in
many Cuban homes. But he won't even be
here! He has to work out of town and
will come back on Christmas Day.

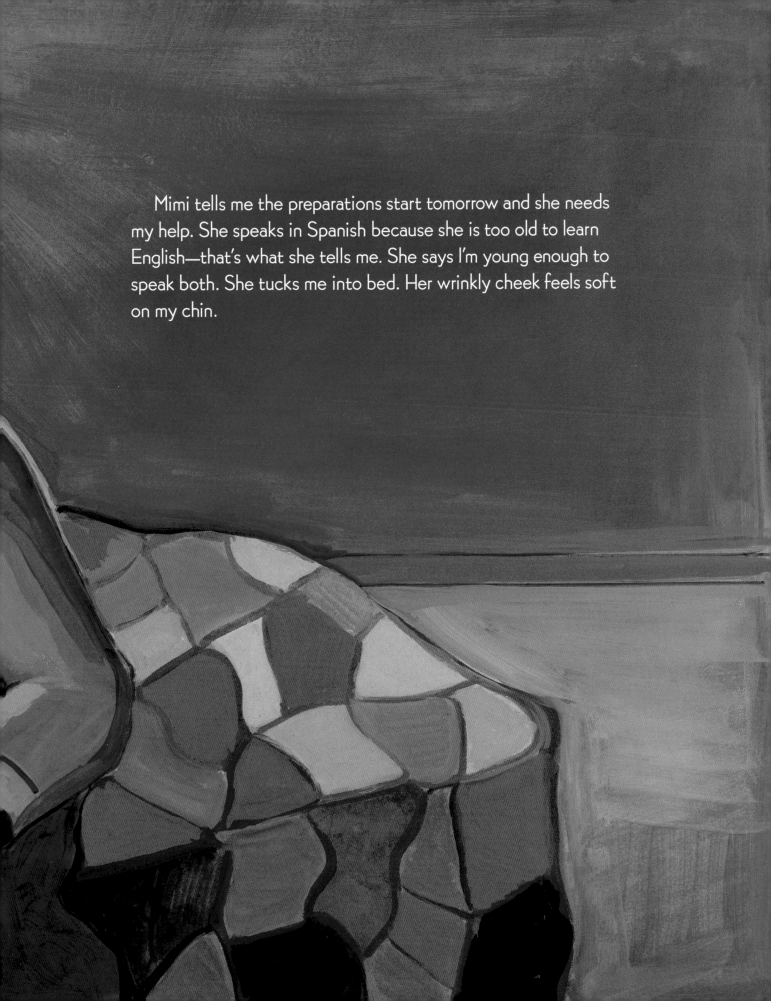

Mimi tells me the preparations start tomorrow and she needs my help. She speaks in Spanish because she is too old to learn English—that's what she tells me. She says I'm young enough to speak both. She tucks me into bed. Her wrinkly cheek feels soft on my chin.

THE NEXT MORNING, SHE WAKES ME AND BRINGS ME

into the kitchen. It is full of women! My aunts and girl cousins stand at the long counter, and everybody works. They peel onions, they chop onions, and they cry. They teach me how to peel the onions. I cry. They laugh.

They sort beans. They peel and chop garlic. Their fingers move so fast, I can barely see what they do. They teach me how to peel garlic. I get little *dedos* of garlic everywhere. They laugh. Mimi whirls around and between us, gathering ingredients and tossing them in a large cast-iron pot. She adds olive oil and sour orange peels and cumin and oregano, and then stirs it all up with a long wooden spoon.

Mimi dips her pinkie into the pot. The women stop chopping and cutting and laughing, hold their breath, and watch her. She pulls out her finger, covered with spicy oil. She smells it, dabs it on her tongue, and smiles. They all exhale and let out a huge laugh. She pours the liquid from the pot into a large glass jar.

"Nina, *mi'jita*, the first batch is ready. Take this jar
of marinade to your uncle Tito's house."

"Where does he live?" I reply in Spanish.

"Just walk out the front door and open your ears."
She hands me the heavy jar, kisses me on the cheek,
and pushes me out of the kitchen.

I walk out the front door. I listen. At first I only hear
the cars going by on *Calle Ocho*. Then I hear a dog barking,
and loud birds above me. I look toward the sound and see
colorful parrots!

Then I hear shouting and laughing. I walk down the street toward the sound, struggling with the jar. The sun is rising, and it feels hotter than yesterday. I see my uncle in the backyard of a house. All my uncles and boy cousins are there. They stand around a huge pit in the ground with a massive fire at the bottom that is burning high into the sky. A few other men gather at a large bathtub back by the fence.

"*¡Vino Nina, mi sobrina, ven acá!*"
Uncle Tito calls me over to him.

He takes the jar from my hands, sets
it on the ground, lifts me in the air, and
twirls me around and around. He smells
like cigar smoke and campfire, and his
bristly chin tickles my cheek.

"Nina, you got tall! You'll be taller
than me soon!" I don't believe him,
because he's really tall, but it makes
me happy.

The men take the marinade. One of them carefully pours it into the bathtub in the backyard. Uncle Tito takes two thick wooden sticks and pushes them deep in the ground on either side of the pit.

"What are you doing?" I ask.

"Well, Nina, I'm making a spit to hold the pig we will roast over the next three days for the *Noche Buena* meal. Hand me that pole!"

I help my cousin Papito carry a long pole over toward Uncle Tito. He holds it over the two wooden sticks and carefully lowers it into the notches. It fits perfectly. All the men cheer!

"Why are they cheering?" I ask Papito. He's my age, but I am taller than he is.

"He's the first one to get the pole into the notches and not drop it into the fire!" Papito replies.

"*Vaya, niña*," says Uncle Tito. "We need more of Mimi's marinade, and you are the only one who can go. Mimi won't let any of us men into the kitchen, and we won't let any of the women by the fire. They need you in the kitchen, but we need you here, too. You will have to go back and forth many times over the next few days."

HE'S RIGHT. FOR THE NEXT THREE DAYS, I peel onions and garlic in the kitchen, my aunts and *abuela* chop them up, and I listen to them tell stories about Cuba.

I bring countless jars of marinade to the men, who pour it over the roasting pig, and I listen to them talk about American football.

All over the neighborhood, other families do the same. On the street between the houses, I meet other boys and girls my age carrying marinade to their uncles. We smell like campfire and garlic.

We taste one another's marinades by dipping our little pinkies into the jars and dabbing them on our tongues. We tell stories about our families and laugh so hard.

We promise to visit each other during *La Noche Buena*.

FINALLY, *LA NOCHE BUENA* ARRIVES.

Feast time! I help my *abuela* set up a table outside as the sun sets and turns the clouds red and orange. Then we change our clothes. I wear a brand-new dress that Mimi gives me. She tells me I look lovely. I tell her she looks beautiful. Then everyone comes: all my aunts wearing colorful dresses, and my uncles dressed in brand-new *guayabera* shirts, with their shoes sparkling. With them come my cousins, also dressed in their best.

Mimi sends me and Papito out to gather fruit from the trees in the neighborhood. We pluck limes for the meat, lemons for the water, avocados for the salad, and mangoes for dessert, all right from the trees to the table.

When we get back
to the table, it is covered
with mounds of food, with
the roasted pig in the center.
Everybody yells and laughs, and
then we all sit down to the feast.

I want to eat right away, but Papito whispers, "We have to wait for the toasts."

The toasts begin, with the best storytellers in the family giving thanks for a great year. Then Mimi, at the head of the table, holds her glass in the air, and the table falls silent. Her big brown eyes glisten as she says, "Let us give thanks to all those here, and those who are not here. We are happy to be alive, and we miss those who are dead, and we are happy that Jesus will be born soon. We are grateful for the pig and this family and the table and the laughter. We are thankful for the laughter."

And then I finally get to eat. It's the most magnificent meal I have ever eaten. I eat plate after plate. Then the neighbors come by, and Mimi feeds them. Afterward, we go to their house, and they feed us. It's a huge traveling party, eaten in many different backyards for many hours. I have never eaten so much, or so well.

Finally, the food is put away, and we all go to the *Misa del Gallo*, the Rooster's Mass, at midnight, where I walk around the church to hug every single member of the congregation, just like everyone else does. By the time we all get back to the house, I am so happy and so tired.

Then Uncle Tito turns on the old record player and grabs my hands, and everyone starts dancing. The music barely stops, but when it does, my aunts and uncles tell more stories and jokes, and as the sun rises on Christmas Day after *La Noche Buena*, the Good Night, everybody finally goes home. Tired but happy.

As my *abuela* tucks me into bed, I ask her, "May I come next year, and can I bring all my up-north cousins?"

She smiles, and says, "*Mi'jita*, nothing would make me happier."

My dad is right. This is the best night of the year, and I can't wait to tell him so.

Y colorín, colorado, este cuento se ha acabado, the end.

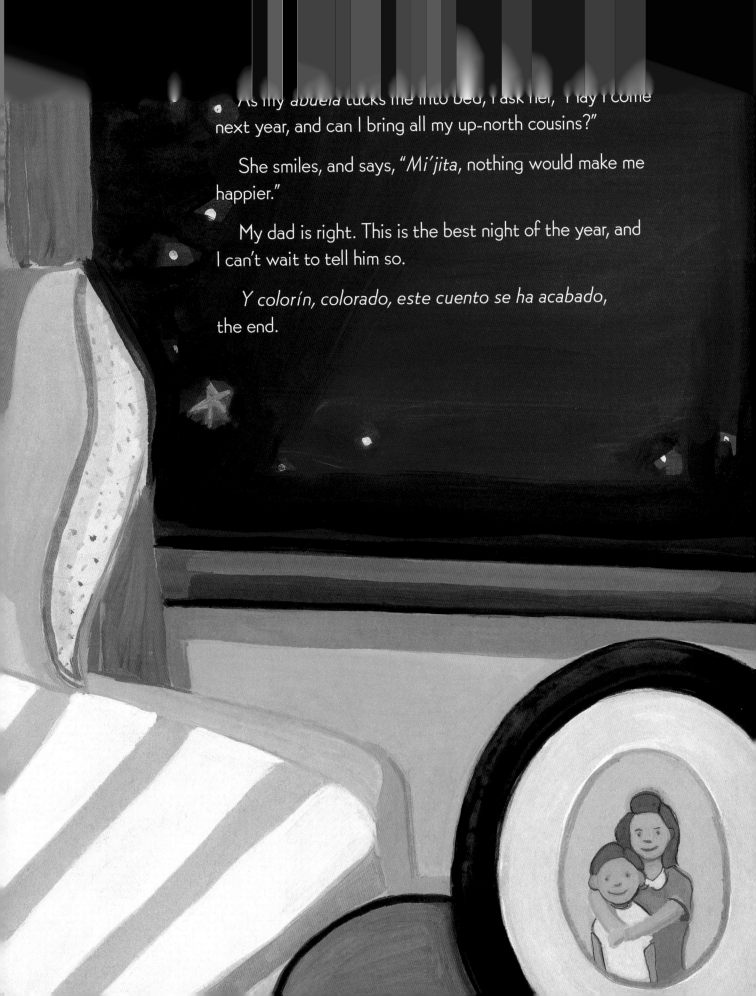

GLOSSARY OF SPANISH WORDS AND PHRASES

LA NOCHE BUENA Literally, "The Good Night," but it is understood to be December 24, Christmas Eve. This night is more celebrated by Cubans than Christmas Day.

ABUELA Grandmother

CALLE OCHO Eighth Street, the main street that runs through the neighborhood of Little Havana, in Miami, Florida, where many Cubans and Cuban Americans live.

DEDOS Literally, "fingers," but here meaning garlic cloves.

MI'JITA A contraction of *mi hija*, a term of endearment meaning "my daughter" or "my girl."

"¡VINO NINA, MI SOBRINA, VEN ACÁ!" "My niece Nina came! Come here!"

"VAYA, NIÑA" "Go, little girl."

GUAYABERA A type of shirt worn by many Cuban men on fancy occasions, with pockets on the front by the waist, and fancy stitching.

Y COLORÍN, COLORADO, ESTE CUENTE SE HA ACABADO This doesn't literally translate. It is a typical and ancient rhyming way in Cuba and Puerto Rico to say "The End" (kind of like "They all lived happily ever after").

ANNALISA ROSE —A. S.   TO MY FAMILY AND FRIENDS. —A. D.

The illustrations in this book were made using acrylic paint on paper.

Cataloging-in-Publication Data has been applied for and may be obtained from the Library of Congress.
ISBN 978-0-8109-8967-2

Text copyright © 2010 Antonio Sacre
Illustrations copyright © 2010 Angela Dominguez
Book design by Chad W. Beckerman

Published in 2010 by Abrams Books for Young Readers, an imprint of ABRAMS. All rights reserved. No portion of this book may be reproduced, stored in a retrieval system, or transmitted in any form or by any means, mechanical, electronic, photocopying, recording, or otherwise, without written permission from the publisher.

Printed and bound in China
10 9 8 7 6 5 4 3 2 1

Abrams Books for Young Readers are available at special discounts when purchased in quantity for premiums and promotions as well as fundraising or educational use. Special editions can also be created to specification. For details, contact specialmarkets@abramsbooks.com or the address below.

ABRAMS
THE ART OF BOOKS SINCE 1949
115 West 18th Street
New York, NY 10011
www.abramsbooks.com